CONTENTS

Pedigree BOOKS

Published by
Pedigree Books Limited
The Old Rectory,
Matford Lane, Exeter,
EX2 4PS
Under licence from Disney
ISBN 1.874507.89.9
© Disney 1997

£6

TOY STORY

REX

Rex is one of the many toys in Andy's bedroom that come to life when no one's around. He's Andy's favourite dinosaur. He's Andy's only dinosaur! He may be a predator, but he's a predator with a soft centre and, like the others, fears being replaced by a newer model.

BO PEEP

Andy uses Bo Peep as the damsel in distress for his Wild West adventure games. Woody always comes to her rescue, so the two are quite close. Of all the toys, she's the most reluctant to believe that Woody would wish another toy harm.

BUZZ AND WOODY

Woody, the cowboy doll, is Andy's favourite toy...until Buzz Lightyear, Space Ranger, comes along! These two rivals for Andy's attention soon learn that they have to look out for each other when they end up in the clutches of Sid, the obnoxious boy next door. Their narrow escape brings them closer together and they're soon best buddies!

SLINKY DOG

Here's a dog with a difference: his body's a slinky! He finds himself stretched to the limit during Buzz and Woody's hair-rasing attempt to get on the removal van and is never the same again!

MR. POTATO HEAD

Often used as the villain in Andy's games, Mr. Potato Head is the first to suspect Woody of trying to get rid of Buzz. The other toys are impressed by his forthright manner and look up to him, often doing as he says. His one wish is to meet Mrs. Potato Head!

Zany Action
on a Crazy
Contraption!
LIGHTYEAR
Disney's
TOY
STORY

Woody the cowboy was Andy's favourite toy. The two would spend hours in Andy's bedroom, going on Wild West adventures together. Woody always saved the day. On this afternoon, he rescued Bo Peep's sheep from One-Eyed Bart, a villain who bore more than a passing resemblance to Mr. Potato Head, another of Andy's favourites.

Andy finished his game and went downstairs to see how his mum was getting on with the party preparations. His birthday wasn't for another week, but the family would be moving house then, so the party had been brought forward. When Woody heard the news, he quickly called the other toys together so he could make an announcement. Birthdays and Christmas were a difficult time for them: they always meant new arrivals.

As the guests began to arrive, the toys watched glumly from the window. There seemed to be so many parcels! The Green Army marched downstairs with the baby monitor to keep everyone informed of Andy's new presents and took up their usual positions.

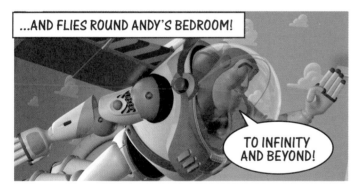

The toys listened intently to the commentary of the presents being opened in the living room below. They sighed with relief as the final present was opened. There had been no gift that posed a threat to any of them. But then Andy's mum brought in her present, and it was huge! Andy tore off the wrapping and all the children began to shout excitedly. The soldiers tried their best, but it was no good. They couldn't see the cause of the fuss.

Andy raced into his room with his new toy, kicking Woody under the bed. Some of his friends followed

him in and they examined the new toy's features. They all thought it was fantastic! Party food soon beckoned, though, so they decided to go back downstairs.Once the children had left the room, the toys came out to meet their new addition. He was a Buzz Lightyear toy, the best money could buy. He had lights, he had lasers - he could even fly!

Woody was the only toy not impressed by Buzz. Even when the Space Ranger took off from the bed and performed a series of somersaults in the air, Woody still didn't think there was anything special about him.

THAT EVENING...

HOW ABOUT DINNER AT PIZZA PLANET?

COOL!

WHILE ANDY GETS READY...

BRRRRRRM!

ANDY'S TAKING ONE TOY WITH HIM...

...WOODY USES THE CAR TO GET RID OF BUZZ!

CRASH!

BUZZ!

THAT WAS NO ACCIDENT.

...HUMPTY DUMPTY WAS PUSHED!

GASP!

ANDY CAN'T FIND BUZZ, SO...

I'LL TAKE WOODY INSTEAD.

MOM, I COULDN'T FIND BUZZ!

I'M SURE HE'S AROUND, HONEY.

AS BUZZ HANGS ON TO THE BACK OF THE CAR...

YOU'LL FIND HIM.

That evening, when all his guests had left, Andy ran back to his room and eagerly played with his new toy. This was the best present ever! It was soon time to eat again, so Andy's mum decided to finish the day with a trip to his favourite restaurant, Pizza Planet. As always, Andy asked if he could take some toys and his mum agreed to let him take just one.

Whilst Andy went to get ready, Woody began to feel a little insecure. He was normally first choice for trips out, but this new Space Ranger had spoilt everything.

What if Andy picked Buzz instead of him? He could hardly bear the thought of being left behind. Feeling that he had to do something, he grabbed Andy's remote-controlled car, or R.C. as he was known. He chuckled to himself as he pushed one button after the other, sending R.C hurtling after the newfangled toy. The car crashed into Buzz, sending him off the windowsill into the garden below.

Woody gasped. What had he done? He really hadn't meant for that to happen, but the other toys were convinced he'd done it on purpose.

THE CAR STOPS FOR PETROL...

...AND BUZZ JUMPS INSIDE.

BUZZ! YOU'RE ALIVE!

I WANT YOU TO KNOW THAT REVENGE IS NOT AN IDEA WE PROMOTE ON MY PLANET.

OH. THAT'S GOOD.

BUT WE'RE NOT ON MY PLANET!

IN THE FIGHT THAT FOLLOWS, THE TWO TUMBLE FROM THE CAR...

IT'S YOUR FAULT WE'RE LOST. YOU PUSHED ME OUT THE WINDOW!

IT'S YOUR FAULT, FOR TURNING UP IN YOUR STUPID SPACESHIP!

A PIZZA PLANET VAN PASSES BY...

HEY, BUZZ! I FOUND ANOTHER SPACESHIP!

AND SOON...

WELCOME TO PIZZA PLANET!

THERE'S ANDY AND MOLLY! BUZZ? WHERE ARE YOU?

WHAT ARE YOU - OH, NO! SID!

Although Woody's prank had gone further than he'd meant it to, it had worked. Andy looked for Buzz, but took his cowboy doll when he couldn't find him. On the way to Pizza Planet, Andy's mum decided to stop for petrol. Woody was just wondering how to explain the accident to the other toys, when Buzz suddenly appeared beside him. At first he was relieved to see the Space Ranger all in one piece, but it was soon clear that the new toy wasn't happy that Woody had tried to 'terminate' him. Buzz was determined to get his own back and threw himself at the surprised cowboy.

As the two were fighting, they fell out of the car, moments before it drove off without them. Gaping at the disappearing vehicle in disbelief, each blamed the other for what had happened. Their argument got more and more furious, until Woody spotted a Pizza Planet delivery van. They could hitch a ride on that!

The van soon caught up with Andy's family, and the two stowaways ran into the restaurant. Once inside, Buzz went missing, only for Woody to find him making friends with the aliens in the Claw Game!

Seeing Andy's obnoxious next door neighbour approaching, Woody leapt inside the game to join Buzz. He was horrified to see Sid guide the claw over the Space Ranger and snap him up. Woody tried pulling Buzz back into the alien pit by tugging at his feet, but the claw was too strong for him and he was pulled out, too. Sid gaped incredulously as he drew out not only a Buzz Lightyear, but a cowboy doll as well!

Sid stuffed his prizes in his rucksack and took them home. Woody was terrified. He'd never been away from Andy before. He had no idea what lay in store for them in the murky depths of Sid's bedroom. When they finally arrived, he and Buzz watched in terror as Sid performed one of his many toy 'operations' on his sister's doll. The mischievous boy ripped the poor dolly's head off and replaced it with that of a pterodactyl, making his sister run sobbing to her mum.

Woody decided he didn't fancy having a head transplant and tried to escape. Bumping into a fellow doll, he asked it for directions.

WOODY SHINES A LIGHT ON THE DOLL...

GASP!

THE NEXT DAY...

WE HAVE WAYS OF MAKING YOU TALK!

SID! YOUR POP TARTS ARE READY!

STILL NO WORD FROM STAR COMMAND.

THE DOOR'S OPEN! WE'RE FREE!

WOODY DIDN'T GET FAR BEFORE...

GULP!

ZZZZZZZZZZZZZ

SSSHH!

MMMM?

GRRRRRRRR!

HE'S AWAKE! SPLIT UP!

THEN...

THE COAST IS CLEAR NOW, BUZZ. BUZZ?

WOULD YOU LIKE SOME TEA?

AS HANNAH GOES DOWNSTAIRS...

LET'S GO! WHAT HAPPENED TO YOU?

ONE MINUTE YOU'RE DEFENDING THE GALAXY, THE NEXT YOU'RE SUCKIN' DOWN DARJEELING!

Woody sensed there was something not quite right about the doll. He shone his torch on it and gasped in disgust. It had only one eye and the body of a meccano spider! Sid was one weird boy!

The next day, Woody was subjected to one of Sid's torturous games and was saved only by breakfast time. He tried another escape, but was stopped in his tracks by the sight of Sid's dog, Scud, lying at the bottom of the stairs. The dog roused and came to investigate, but Woody and Buzz had already hidden from him. Buzz tried to fly

but misjudged his landing and crashed in a heap on the floor, losing an arm in the process.

Once Scud had disappeared, Woody went to look for Buzz. Hannah had found him and was subjecting him to a dolls' tea party! Waiting until she left the room, Woody went to see if Buzz was all right. His fall had affected him and he was talking nonsense, but Woody hoped it would soon pass. It was then that Woody had an idea. If they went to the window, they could shout to the toys in Andy's house!

11

WOODY ATTRACTS THE ATTENTION OF HIS FRIENDS IN THE OPPOSITE HOUSE...

HEY, GUYS!

IT'S WOODY! HE'S IN THE PSYCHO'S BEDROOM!

HERE! CATCH THIS!

AFTER WHAT YOU DID TO BUZZ?

BUZZ IS JUST FINE. LOOK!

NOW HELP US OUTTA HERE!

GASP!

MURDERER! I HOPE SID PULLS YOUR VOICE BOX OUT!

NO! WAIT!

THANKS FOR YOUR HELP, BUZZ.

GO AWAY, YOU FREAKS!

THEN...

BUZZ, GET UP! SID'S COMING! USE YOUR LEGS!

Woody climbed up to Sid's bedroom window and was delighted to see his friends opposite. He shouted to them to attract their attention, then threw a them string of Christmas lights: if they tied the end to something, he and Buzz could easily climb along it to safety. The toys were suspicious of Woody, though, especially Mr. Potato Head. They hadn't forgotten that he'd pushed Buzz from the window. They demanded to know that Buzz was all right before they agreed to help. Woody tried to get the Space Ranger to come to the window, but he was still delirious. In desperation, he held up Buzz's arm as proof that he was

there, but when the toys saw that Buzz wasn't on the end of it, they all gasped at Woody's brutality. They turned their backs in disgust and refused to co-operate.

Suddenly, there was panic. The toys in Sid's bedroom could hear their master coming up the stairs. Woody tried to pull Buzz into a hiding place, but the Space Ranger had lost the use of his legs, although the other toys had mended his arm. Unable to drag him any further, Woody had to abandon his efforts and leave Buzz behind. He rushed to hide and waited with dread for Sid to come in.

WOODY FINDS A PLACE TO HIDE...

SORRY, BUZZ.

I'M GONNA SEND THIS SPACEMAN INTO ORBIT!

WOODY IS HELPLESS AS SID TIES BUZZ TO THE ROCKET...

BUT...

AH, MAN. LAUNCH DELAYED DUE TO ADVERSE WEATHER CONDITIONS!

WHILE SID SLEEPS...

PSST! BUZZ! SEE IF YOU CAN GET THIS TOOL BOX OFF HERE!

NEXT MORNING...

COME ON, SHERIFF! THERE'S A KID IN THAT HOUSE WHO NEEDS US!

BUT SID WAKES UP AND RUNS OFF TO LAUNCH BUZZ...

WE GOTTA SAVE BUZZ, GUYS. HE'S THE ONLY FRIEND I'VE GOT!

SO...

WHAT WAS THAT?

Woody watched helplessly as Sid burst into the room with a new 'toy': a highly dangerous rocket. Sid gleefully strapped Buzz to the huge firework with the intention of launching him into space, but had to abandon his plans when he saw it was raining. He decided to try again the next day.

That night, as Sid slept, Woody called to Buzz. Sid had put a tool box on top of his hiding place, so he was trapped. If Buzz helped him, he could remove the rocket and they could escape together. Buzz, however, sat glumly

where he was. He felt that he was a failure - he couldn't even fly without messing it up! What good was a Space Ranger that couldn't fly properly? Woody spent the night telling Buzz that he was really a cool toy and that Andy needed him.

Suddenly, Buzz sprang into action, but the noise of the box falling to the floor woke Sid. Remembering his plan, he picked up Buzz and sped into the garden with him. Woody gathered the toys together. Freaks though he thought they were, he needed their help.

The toys decided to teach Sid a lesson and thought up an ingenious plan. A toy called Ducky sneaked down the air duct to ring the doorbell. While Hannah and Scud went to see who was there, Woody and the others raced through the kitchen and out through the dog flap in the back door. They looked for Sid and saw that he had his match poised under the rocket - there was no time to lose! Woody spoke as loud as he could, making Sid pick him up curiously. The toys saw their moment and wreaked their revenge on their owner, making him flee, screaming, into the house.

Woody and Buzz thanked Sid's toys for their help and rushed over to Andy's house, only to be deeply disappointed. It was the day of the move and Andy's car was disappearing down the road. They still had a chance: the removal van.

Buzz jumped aboard and tried to help Woody up, but Scud was on the loose. The dog began to chase the truck, barking furiously. Woody's dangling legs were irresistible, and he jumped up at them as he ran. Finally getting one leg between his teeth, he tugged at it fiercely.

Now it was Buzz's turn to rescue Woody. He leaped off the van on to Scud's nose, confusing the dog and leaving Woody to scramble safely aboard. Inside the van, Woody looked frantically for Andy's toy box and ripped it open. Ignoring the toys' gasps, he found R.C. and directed him towards Buzz. The toys were furious that Woody was hurling toys overboard, just as he had with Buzz back at the house. Woody had no chance to explain and was given what the toys thought was some of his own medicine. They all grabbed hold of him and threw him off the back of the truck.

Having left Scud in the middle of a car pile-up, Buzz and R.C. picked Woody up as he fell from the van. It was only then that the toys saw Woody had been trying to help. Feeling ashamed of what they had done, they watched helplessly as R.C.'s batteries ran out and he slowed down to a stop. Now they might never see them again!

Buzz had an idea: he was still carrying the powerful rocket on his back. If Woody lit it, they would easily catch up with the truck!

WHOOOOSH!

NEXT STOP.. ANDY!

LOOK! HERE'S WOODY AND BUZZ, COMING UP FAST!

I CAN'T HOLD ON ANY LONGER!

SO...

AARGH! THIS IS THE PART WHERE WE BLOW UP!

BUZZ RELEASES THE ROCKET JUST IN TIME...

BOOM!

THIS ISN'T FLYING, IT'S FALLING WITH STYLE!

HEY, BUZZ! WE'RE FLYING!

BUZZ, WE'RE GONNA MISS THE TRUCK!

WE'RE NOT AIMING FOR THE TRUCK!

HA! TO INFINITY AND BEYOND!

Woody and Buzz waited apprehensively for the rocket to take off, then WHOOSH! They were hurled forward in an explosive burst and sped towards the van. Andy's toys spotted the bright flame in the distance and craned their necks to see what was happening. The force of the rocket was a little too strong, though, and Woody found it impossible to hold on to R.C. He let go, sending himself and Buzz up into the sky. R.C., left on the ground, was still travelling under the momentum of the rocket and went hurtling back into the van. Woody began to panic as it dawned on him that the rocket would blow up shortly,

but Buzz was already prepared. He released it from his back seconds before it exploded and began to fly, keeping a firm hold on Woody.

Woody yelled in terror and covered his eyes, but fear soon turned to excitement when he realised that Buzz was really flying. It was true, this guy was a Space Ranger! He giggled as they glided through the air down towards the traffic below. They spotted the van, but Buzz's plan was not to return to it, but to land in Andy's car. It wouldn't be long before they were all together again!

Buzz's aim was right on target and the two fell through the car's sun roof, plopping into a box next to Andy. Andy looked at the box and gasped. He'd been searching high and low for Buzz and Woody, and there they were, right beside him in the car! He snatched them up and hugged them to his chest, shouting to his mum that his favourite toys had turned up, just as she said they would. Now he couldn't wait to get to the new house!

The months went by and Andy and his toys settled into their new home. Before they knew it, there was snow on the ground and Christmas had arrived again. The toys dreaded Christmas: the threat of new toys coming to replace them was even greater than on birthdays! The Green Army men carried out their usual manoeuvre of relaying to the other toys what presents the children had received. They all listened and were relieved to hear that one of the presents was a Mrs. Potato Head - just what Mr. Potato Head had been waiting for!

Buzz and Woody weren't too worried. They would always be Andy's favourites...wouldn't they?

WHICH WOODY?

All the shadows below look the same, but only one exactly matches this picture of Woody. Which one?
The answer is at the bottom of the page.

Answer: Number 3

BRICKS MIX

Andy has used Molly's bricks to spell out the names of his favourite toys, but someone's jumbled them all up! Help Bo Peep to put them back in order again.
The answers are at the bottom of the page.

D O W O Y

T H O D R A P T A M O E

G L O K N I Y D S

B L I G T R E A Y H Z U Z

Answers: Woody, Mr. Potato Head, Slinky Dog, Buzz Lightyear.

ARMY ANTICS

The Green Army soldiers are out on another mission! If you match up all the pairs of soldiers here, you'll have one leftover. Which is the odd commando out? The answer is at the bottom of the page.

Answer: Number 8.

20

MARTIAN ATTACK

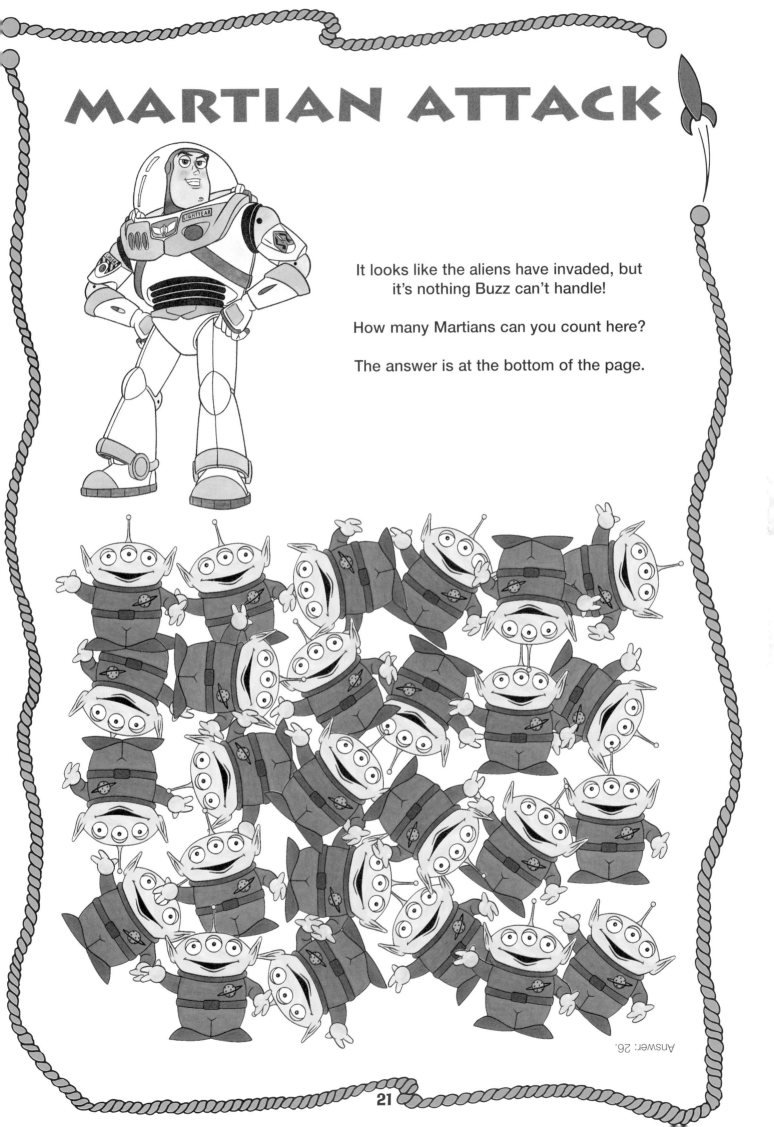

It looks like the aliens have invaded, but it's nothing Buzz can't handle!

How many Martians can you count here?

The answer is at the bottom of the page.

Answer: 26.

HERCULES

PEGASUS

This beautiful winged horse was a gift to baby Hercules from his father, Zeus. The two spent years apart while Hercules was growing up on earth, but their friendship survived until their reunion on Mount Olympus.

PHILOCTETES

Phil for short, this bandy-legged little goat-man is a retired trainer of heroes and lives on the misty island of Idra. Hercules asks him for help and manages to persuade him to dust off his training gear to help him become a hero.

ZEUS

The father of Hercules, Zeus is the thunderbolt-wielding King of the Gods. He was devastated when his newborn baby son was kidnapped and taken down to earth.

BABY HERCULES

This blond bundle of fun was the most powerful of all the gods - until Pain and Panic came along, that is.

TEENAGE HERCULES

The cute baby grew into a clumsy teenager who feels out of place on earth and seeks his true identity on Mount Olympus.

HADES

This evil god sent his demon helpers, Pain and Panic, to kidnap Hercules and make him immortal.

Many years ago, in the faraway land of Ancient Greece, there lived many powerful gods and extraordinary heroes. Hercules was the son of Zeus, the King of the Gods, but was cruelly snatched from his parents as a baby and left on earth to lead life as a mere mortal.

Hercules, though, still had extraordinary strength. As he grew into an awkward teenager, he soon realised that he wasn't like other boys of his age. Things would happen when he was around. One day he managed to destroy the whole market place, just by trying to catch a flying discus! People called him a freak and did their best to avoid him. Hercules became more and more unhappy and felt as if he didn't belong...

Alcmene and Amphitryon had found the abandoned baby Hercules almost eighteen years earlier. It had been in the middle of a fierce storm, when Zeus's anguished tears at the loss of his child fell to earth in torrents. Although the couple could see from his gold medallion that Hercules had come from the gods, they believed he had merely been sent as an answer to their prayers. They had no idea that he had been kidnapped by Pain and Panic, and that the demons had been in the middle of trying to poison him.

Alcmene and Amphitryon had never told Hercules about his background. But when they saw how unhappy he was, they knew they couldn't keep it from him much longer. One day, as Amphitryon listened to Hercules pouring out his feelings, he decided the time had come to tell his son the truth. As the couple had feared, Hercules immediately decided that he would have to make the journey to Mount Olympus to find out who he really was. Hercules thanked his tearful parents for all their kindness, then set off for the Temple of Zeus.

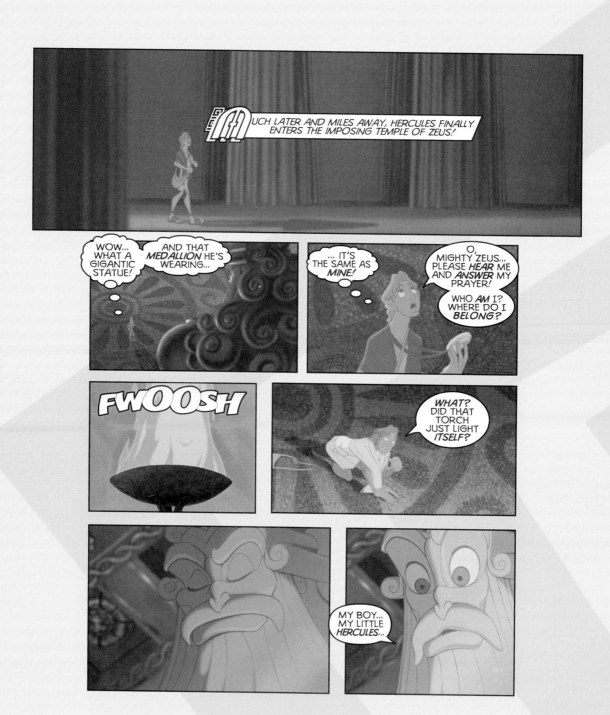

When Hercules finally reached Mount Olympus, he gazed up in awe at the huge temple. Taking a deep breath, he entered and saw in front of him a towering statue that wore a medallion just like his own. He dropped his bag and knelt before the figure, praying that he be told the truth. Suddenly, the rush of an ignited flame broke the silence. Hercules swung round to see who had lit the nearby torch, but was astonished to find that he was still alone. As he looked back at the statue, there was a clap of thunder and a lightning bolt. Hercules shielded his eyes, then gasped in dismay as the giant figure began to come to life. It was Zeus!

Hercules stared open-mouthed at the gigantic King of the Gods. When Zeus eventually spoke, Hercules yelled in terror and tried to escape. The figure had called him by name. How did he know who he was? And didn't he just call him his 'little boy'? He was beginning to regret that he'd ever left the safety of his cosy farmhouse on earth!

Zeus smiled as his son scuttled towards the door. He leaned over and effortlessly picked up the struggling boy in his huge hand, trying to reassure him as he did so. It was only when he heard the word 'father' that Hercules stopped to listen. He stared up at Zeus's face in disbelief. His father was the King of the Gods! As Zeus made affectionate comments about how much his son had grown, a hundred questions rushed into Hercules's head. The first thing that struck him was that if his father was a god, he himself must be one! Then he wanted to know why his parents had given him away as a baby. Zeus explained that he and his wife had loved their baby son more than anything and that they were devastated when he was taken from them by evil forces.

Now all Hercules needed to know was how to become a god again. Zeus explained that if he could prove himself a true hero on earth, his godhood would be restored. To do that, he had to seek out Philoctetes, the trainer of heroes.

Eager to start his search for Philoctetes, Hercules turned to go, but his father stopped him. Zeus put his fingers to his lips and whistled. Within seconds, a beautiful winged horse had flown into the temple and given Hercules a friendly lick. Hercules smiled and, as he stroked the horse's coat, he remembered: the horse was called Pegasus and was a gift from his father when he was born. Now he had a friend to travel with! After promising his father that he would not disappoint him, Hercules climbed on to Pegasus's back and the two set off for the Isle of Idra. With a tear in his eye, Zeus wished them luck and waved as the boy and his horse disappeared into the clouds.

The next day, Hercules and Pegasus descended through the morning mist and landed on the island. It was overgrown and shabby, with remnants of statues scattered here and there. Hercules slid down from his horse's back and wandered round, gazing at the mess and wondering whether he was in the right place. Suddenly, the silence was broken by the sound of nearby giggling.

HEE HEE HEE

BA-A-AH! BA-AH!

HEE HEE -- OH!

HERCULES SEES THREE NYMPHS FROLICKING...AND WHAT APPEARS TO BE A *GOAT* STUCK IN THE *BUSHES!*

BUT WHEN HE TRIES TO FREE THE *"GOAT"*...

WHOA! HEY, BUTT OUT, BUDDY -- GET YOUR OWN SPOT!

WHO *ARE* YOU, ANYWAY?

YA SCARED THE *NYMPHS* AWAY!

WHATSAMATTA, YA NEVER SEEN A *SATYR* BEFORE?

UH...NO. CAN YOU *HELP* ME?

I'M LOOKING FOR SOMEONE CALLED *PHILOCTETES.* HE'S A GREAT *HERO*-TRAINER.

Hercules was curious to find out who else was on the island and walked over to the bushes where the laughter was coming from. Pulling back the foliage, he saw some nymphs dancing around. As he watched them play, he realised that he could hear another sound, like bleating. Looking round for an animal, he spotted what he thought was a goat stuck in the bushes and, trying to help, pulled him out by his back legs and lifted him up. To his astonishment, the animal's top half was that of a fat little man with horns!

The creature was most annoyed that Hercules had interfered and spoiled his view of the nymphs, who had now trotted shyly away. He shouted abuse at the puzzled Hercules and wriggled crossly from the boy's grasp, then looked at him expectantly and demanded to know who he was. After a little hesitation, Hercules cleared his throat and explained that he was on the island to find Philoctetes, trainer of heroes. If the little goatman could just point him in the right direction, he wouldn't trouble him again.

–SIGH–
CALL ME **PHIL.**

PHIL? WOW!

BOY, AM I GLAD TO MEET **YOU!**

I'M HERCULES, AND THIS IS **PEGASUS.**

I NEED **YOUR HELP!** I WANT TO BECOME A **TRUE HERO.**

SORRY, KID. CAN'T HELP YA. SEE...

...I'M **RETIRED.**

LOOK, I **GOTTA** DO THIS.

HAVEN'T YOU EVER HAD A **DREAM?** SOMETHING YOU WANTED SO BAD YOU'D DO **ANYTHING?**

YEAH.

C'MON **INSIDE,** KID.

I'LL SHOW YA WHAT HAPPENED TO **MY** DREAM.

I'LL WARN YA **NOW,** THOUGH...

...IT **AIN'T** PRETTY.

WOW -- **LOOK** AT THIS STUFF!

"**ARGO**"...

...WAIT... THIS IS THE MAST FROM **THE** ARGO?

The creature sighed wearily and admitted that he was Philoctetes, but they could call him Phil. Hercules was surprised, since Phil wasn't at all what he had expected, but he was also delighted that he had found him so soon after arriving on the island. Giving Phil's hand a hearty shake, he introduced himself and Pegasus, then explained that he was looking for some training. He wanted to become a true hero! Phil rolled his eyes and turned away, then began to walk back to his house. Hercules gazed after him expectantly, waiting for an answer.

Hercules was disappointed to hear Phil refuse his request. The trainer explained that he was now retired and went to open his door, but Hercules stopped him. He begged Phil to think again; he was desperate to realise his dream and he couldn't do it on his own. Phil could see that Hercules wasn't going to give up easily and led him into his home. The boy followed and stared in awe at the swords, shields, paintings and sculptures of the universe's greatest heroes that filled the room. This was more of a museum than a home!

Phil turned to Hercules and told him that he had trained many great heroes in his time, but they had all let him down in the end. That was why he had decided to retire from training altogether. He pointed to a statue of Achilles, the greatest Greek warrior in the Trojan War. Hercules recognised the figure and knew all about him. When he was a baby, Achilles' mother dipped him in a magical river, hoping to make him immortal. The spot where she held him by the heel had remained untouched by the water, leaving him mortal.

Phil told Hercules how Achilles had everything that it took to be a hero: he had great strength, he was fast and he could fight well. But his heel was his weakness. To demonstrate his point, Phil gave the heel of the statue a light flick with his finger, bringing the whole figure crashing to the floor. All that training had been wasted. Hercules looked sadly at the crumbled remains. Phil had similar stories to tell of all the other 'heroes' he'd trained and made it clear he could not go through such disappointment again.

Phil insisted that he knew only too well what it was like to have broken dreams and again told Hercules that he couldn't help him. Hercules, though, was determined to show Phil that he was different, that he could be a hero. In desperation, he grabbed Phil's arm and dragged him out of the door, promising to show him what he could do. He looked around, then walked over to the enormous stone arm and shield of a broken statue. With very little effort, he picked it up and raised it above his head before hurling it into the sea as if it were a pebble.

Phil was astonished at such a show of strength and watched wide-eyed as the statue remnant sank beneath the waves. He thought for a moment and almost considered changing his mind, then declared he was too old to go back to hero training. He tried to walk away, but stopped in his tracks when Hercules mentioned his father's name. Phil was taken aback for a moment and stared at the gawky teenager before him. This couldn't possibly be the son of the King of the Gods, 'Mr. Lightning Bolts'...could it?

Phil looked Hercules up and down once more and decided that the boy must be lying. He was cross with himself for almost believing such an obvious ploy to get him to change his mind. The sneer returned to his face and he scoffed at Hercules, insisting again that he would not help him, even if he really was who he said he was. As Hercules and Pegasus looked at each other sadly, Phil's outburst was suddenly interrupted by a tremendous bolt of lightning that seemed to whiten the whole universe with a deafening crash.

Everyone was blinded for a few moments after the lightning had struck. Hercules rubbed his eyes to try and get them back to normal and when he opened them again, he saw Phil before him, stunned into a frazzled silence. He realised that his father must have been listening to the whole conversation and smiled to himself as he waited for Phil to speak. The blackened little goatman eventually recovered and was now glad to offer his help. He wasn't, after all, in any position to argue with the King of the Gods!

Phil resigned himself to coming out of retirement, then cheered himself with the thought that perhaps some good might come of it: perhaps Hercules really would turn out to be a true hero and his life as a trainer would not have been wasted. He set the boy to work and made sure he spent every day in training. Hercules ran, he jumped, he did sit-ups, he did pull-ups, all under Phil's watchful eye. He even had to do press-ups with Phil and Pegasus on his back! Hercules also had to learn to control his clumsiness, so balancing exercises were part of the regime, too.

From time to time, Phil measured the young hero's biceps, but they weren't yet big enough. The training had to continue, harder than before. Not only did Hercules have to exercise, he had other heroes' skills to learn, too: archery, damsel saving and sword throwing were all part of the regime. He even had a go at Phil throwing, which he enjoyed most of all the sports he tried! Phil was soon glad to be teaching again: Hercules was a dedicated pupil and trained religiously day and night for years.

For a long time, Hercules awoke in the mornings and hoped that this would be his 'hero' day, then went to bed in the evenings even more determined to work harder. Finally, the day came. Standing on a tree stump, Phil measured the biceps of the fully-grown Hercules and was impressed. He was now satisfied that not only did this young man have enough strength to become a hero, he had also learnt to control it properly. The clumsy, gawky teenager who didn't know where he belonged had over the years become a confident, skillful adult who knew exactly where he was going: The Temple of Zeus on Mount Olympus.

First, though, Hercules had to put his skills to use and prove that he really was a true hero. He couldn't wait! He was desperate to fight some monsters, save some damsels...anything! Phil tried to calm his excitable pupil, but agreed to take him for a 'road test'. The two men climbed on to Pegasus's back and they all set off for the city of Thebes...but that's another story!

BITS AND PIECES

Uh-oh. Hercules has done it again! He's knocked over some vases and has to try and put them together again. How many complete vases like the one shown can he make from the broken parts? The answer is at the bottom of the page.

Answer: 4 Vases.

THE ROAD TO OLYMPUS

Hercules is going in search of his real parents.
To do that, he would have to make his way to Olympus.
Which way would he go?
The answer is at the bottom of the page.

37

MATCH THE LOST POSSESSIONS

Below are some of the characters you have just met in the Hercules story.
Can you draw a line from each character to their lost possession?
Look back at the story if you're not sure!
The answers are at the bottom of the page.

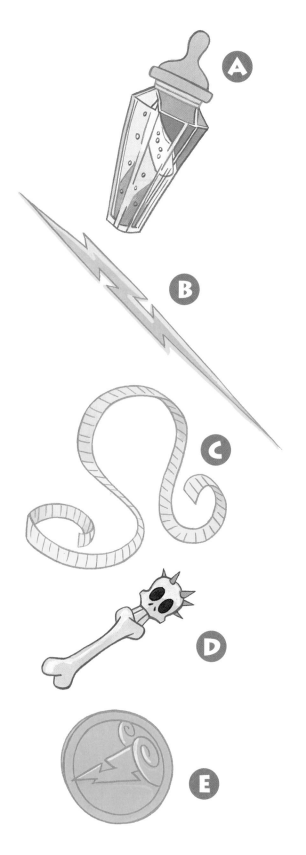

Answer: A5, B4, C1, D2, E3

SPOT WHAT'S WRONG

Zeus and Hera are delighted with Hercules, their new baby son. Look at this picture carefully and see if you can spot the seven things that wouldn't have been around when Hercules was born all those years ago! The answers are at the bottom of the page.

THE Little Mermaid

Ariel

Ariel the little mermaid lives in the undersea city of Atlantis with her sisters and father, King Triton. Ever curious, she never tires of exploring the ocean depths and is particularly fond of the 'human treasures' that she finds in sunken shipwrecks.

Flounder

Flounder the brightly-coloured guppy is Ariel's best friend. He is both scared and fascinated by the little mermaid's adventures, but will always stick by her in an emergency.

Sebastian

Sebastian the crab is Ariel's long-suffering tutor. King Triton often asks him to keep an eye on his daughter, but the old crab only seems to become entangled in her escapades!

King Triton

King Triton is the powerful but kindly ruler of Atlantis. He is very protective of his youngest daughter, Ariel, and has trouble understanding 'teenage stuff'. He's often concerned by her interest in humans.

Ursula

This tentacled sea-witch lives in a murky cave at the bottom of the ocean and is determined to one day take King Triton's place as ruler of the sea. She is helped in her unsuccessful plots by her wicked eels, Flotsam and Jetsam.

40

Disney's

THE LITTLE MERMAID

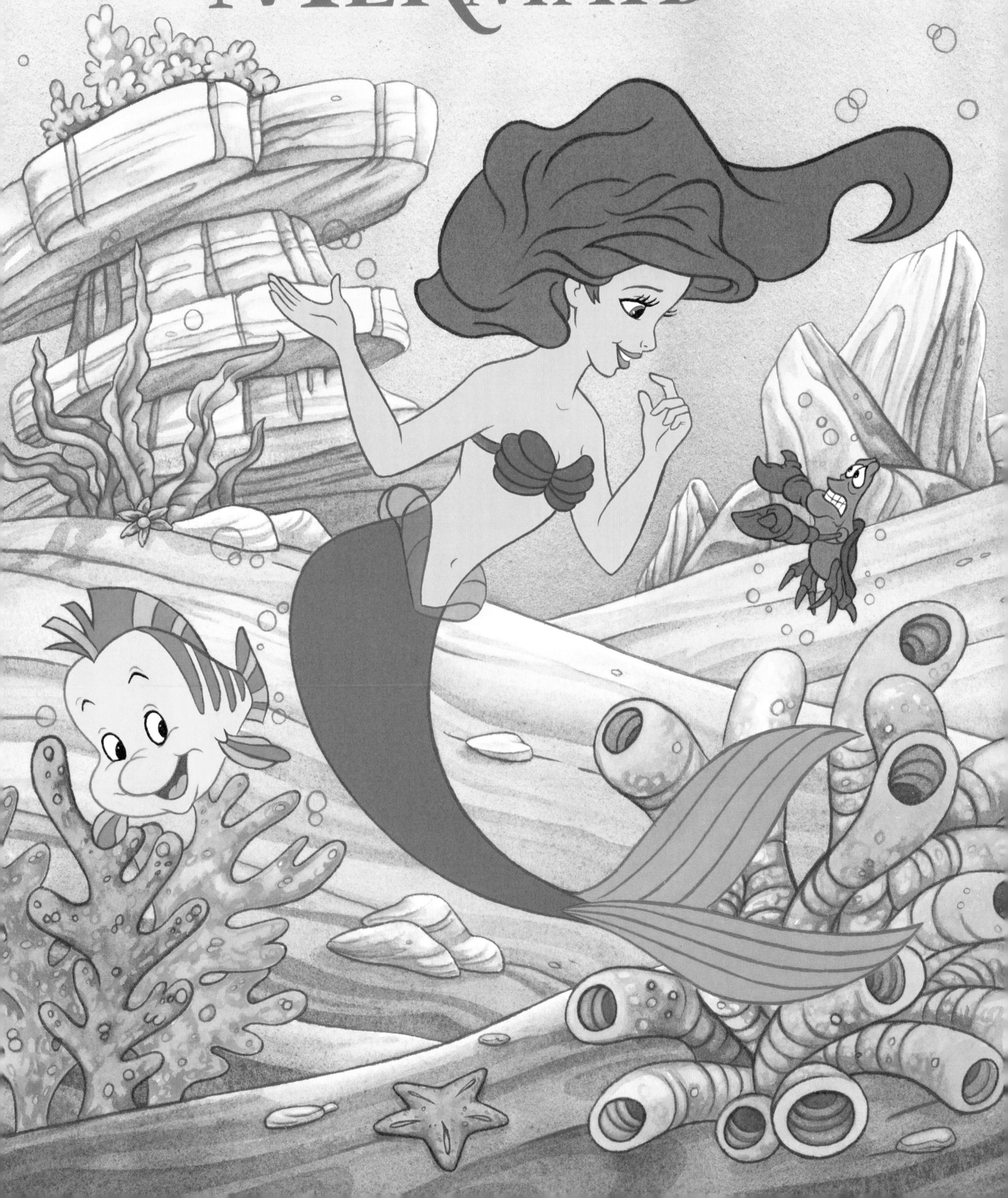

Rosy, a little mermaid, lived deep down in the ocean, a few miles away from the great undersea kingdom of Atlantis. Her aunt lived in Atlantis and would often tell stories about life there with King Triton and his beautiful daughter, Princess Ariel. Rosy was always asking to come and stay and her aunt promised that she would invite her soon.

Finally, the day arrived for Rosy's visit. She could hardly wait for her aunt to come and pick her up and was ready an hour early. She was delighted when she eventually spotted her aunt in the distance, travelling with her baby twins in a huge, dolphin-drawn shell. Rosy hopped aboard and they set off for the famous city.

WELCOME TO THE PALACE, ROSY!

WHAT WAS THAT? WELL, WHY DON'T YOU ASK HIM?

YOU WANT TO KNOW WHICH ONE'S ARIEL, DON'T YOU?

ROSY'S HEARD SO MUCH ABOUT HER THAT SHE CAN'T WAIT TO MEET HER!

HELLO! I'M ARIEL. I'VE BEEN LOOKING FORWARD TO MEETING YOU, TOO.

REALLY? THANKS!

HAVE A LITTLE REST, THEN AS SOON AS DAD'S GONE I'LL SHOW YOU ROUND.

WATCH YOURSELF WITH THIS LITTLE RASCAL, ROSY!

After two hours of crossing the sea-bed through shoals of fish and forests of sea-weed, Rosy could make out the city of Atlantis in the distance. On their arrival, her aunt drove them straight to the Coral Palace to meet everyone. Rosy gasped as she stared up at the stately Royal Palace. It was beautiful! King Triton came out to greet them and was very welcoming. Rosy, though, was desperate to meet Princess Ariel and looked at all the young mermaids gathered there, trying to guess which one she was.

A young mermaid with red hair swam forward and scooped up the baby twins in her arms, giving them a big hug. She smiled at Rosy and introduced herself as Ariel, adding that she had also been looking forward to the visit. Rosy grinned back, proud that a princess should want to meet her. Returning the twins to their mother, Ariel promised her new friend a tour of the city, just as soon as her father had gone back into the palace. King Triton decided to leave the girls to do as they wished and went off to attend to royal business.

Before the mermaids could spend the rest of the day together, the twins needed feeding. The babies were tired and hungry after travelling all morning, so Rosy went to help her aunt give them some lunch and put them down to sleep. Ariel waited nearby and thought about the best places she could take Rosy to later. She wanted her new friend to go home with a good impression of Atlantis, not to mention unusual souvenirs. Her plans were soon interrupted by Rosy's unexpected return. A little concerned, she asked what was wrong.

Rosy told Ariel that her aunt needed some help and asked her to lend a hand. Ariel smiled knowingly, suspecting that the twins were being mischievous, as usual. They were quite a handful at the best of times, but got particularly excitable if their routine was disrupted. Ariel followed Rosy until she found the babies' flustered mother, who had her head in her hands and was desperately trying to get the twins under control. She was raising her voice to them and pleading with them to behave, but the boys paid no attention to her.

Ariel watched the two babies running riot around the sea-bed and chuckled to herself. They were chasing fish and climbing rocks and ripping up sea-weed by the roots. In fact, they were making complete nuisances of themselves, and however much their mother chased and scolded, they carried on regardless, giggling as they went. Rosy looked at Ariel worriedly, but seeing her expression began to smile, too. She felt sorry for her poor aunt, but she had to admit that her little cousins were very entertaining to watch!

As Ariel swam to and fro and helped to catch the twins, their mother explained why she was getting so cross. She had a long list of things to do, but she had no one to look after the children and they were being so difficult! Ariel smiled, as one baby tried to wriggle free from her arms. She knew that the babies were just being babies. They were over-tired and needed some rest, so she picked them up and offered to take them out for a walk round the palace gardens. The gentle rocking of the pram would soon send them to sleep.

Ariel tucked up the twins in their little shell-shaped pram, then rocked and swayed them round the gardens until they drifted off into a contented sleep, sucking their thumbs. She was pleased that her plan had worked, and Rosy was even happier: now they could get on with some sightseeing! They left the pram amongst some clumps of sea-weed and went off to explore. Ariel showed Rosy the most beautiful parts of the city, including the spectacular coral beds where they could get some souvenir coral pieces to take back with them.

When the mermaids returned to the spot where they'd left the pram, though, Ariel let out a scream. The covers had been thrown off the pram and it was empty! Rosy gasped and wondered what they should do next. Ariel frowned slightly and looked around her. The twins couldn't have got far, they were only little. They had probably wandered off on one of their games. She spotted a trail of bubbles leading off into the distance and decided they should follow it. Hopefully, the babies would be at the end of it!

Ariel and Rosy swam as fast as they could along the bubble trail, but stopped short at the edge of an abyss. They peered down into the murky waters, but could see nothing. They exchanged worried glances. What if the twins had swum down there? Even worse, what if someone or something had taken them down there? Ariel knew she would have to swim down there herself to find out. She had to get the twins back safely. Rosy admired Ariel's boldness and decided that they would descend into the dark abyss together.

Ariel plunged headlong down the bank first, then Rosy followed. Ariel warned her friend to stay close by in case anything happened. Her father often warned her not to swim down there, since no one knew what fierce creatures were lurking in the ocean depths, but she hardly ever listened to her father and besides, this was an emergency. Rosy sensed that there may be danger ahead and felt a mixture of fear and excitement. Deeper and deeper the mermaids swam, until they could make out another sandy bed in the distance.

The two mermaids came to a stop behind a rock and looked down at the ocean bed below. Ariel touched Rosy's arm and pointed out some lights shining several feet away in the sand. Rosy wondered what they were and was astonished when the lights began to move closer. Ariel didn't seem concerned by them and it was soon clear why: they were coming from a group of fish! Each fish had a small lantern at the end of its spiky back fin, to light its path through the dim waters of the abyss. Rosy had never seen such fish at home and stared after them in awe as

they swam away. She wondered what other surprises Atlantis had in store.

Suddenly, Ariel shuddered slightly and rubbed her arms. The water here was colder than at the palace and she remembered her father's warning about going into the abyss. Feeling a little afraid, she urged Rosy to turn back: the twins weren't here. Rosy was about to follow, when she grabbed Ariel's arm and pulled her over to another distant rock.

I DON'T KNOW. I'VE NEVER SEEN FISH LIKE THAT BEFORE!

THEY'RE UGLY, AREN'T THEY? LET'S HOPE THEY DON'T SPOT US!

BUT...

HUH? OH, NO! GO AWAY!

HEY!

HELLO! HI!

ARIEL AND ROSY ARE IN TROUBLE...

WHY WERE YOU SPYING ON US? WHO ARE YOU?

HELP!

Rosy had spotted something moving behind the rock. She and Ariel peeped over the top and gasped at what they saw. Two enormous, ugly, bloated fish bobbed around in the water before them. They were shaped like huge maggots and covered in spines, and their white bodies seemed to glow a little. Neither of the girls had seen anything like them before, and whispered to each other to avoid attracting attention. Some small fish had seen the girls and, trying to be friendly, called out a greeting to them. Ariel tried to shoo them away, but it was too late.

The strange fish had heard and were coming to investigate.

The monster fish were suspicious of the mermaids and accused them of spying, grabbing hold of them with their strong, blue fins. Ariel and Rosy cried out for help, but no one could hear them so far down in the the ocean. The maggoty creatures gripped them both as they tried to wriggle free and demanded to know who they were. The little fish that had caused all the commotion with their greetings hurried away in fear.

49

AND SO... YOU TWO WILL STAY LOCKED IN HERE UNTIL WE'VE DECIDED WHAT TO DO WITH YOU!

UM...THEY DON'T LOOK DANGEROUS, BUT WE HAD BETTER KEEP AN EYE ON THEM!

NEARBY, THE TWINS ARE GETTING WORRIED. WHERE HAVE ARIEL AND ROSY DISAPPEARED TO?

ARIEL?

MEANWHILE... THE CHILDREN CAN'T BE HERE. WE WOULD HAVE HEARD THEM.

WHAT WILL HAPPEN TO US, ARIEL?

BUT... ARIEL! ROSY! THE TWINS!

Ariel and Rosy were taken to a nearby cave and locked in. As they huddled together, they were told that they would remain there until it was decided what should be done with them. Ariel comforted Rosy and assured her that the fish were probably not dangerous. Nevertheless, she began to think of a way to escape.

The twins, meanwhile, had begun to look for the two mermaids. They had earlier escaped to the abyss when they awoke to find themselves alone, but had been quietly

playing hide and seek when Ariel and Rosy had gone past in search of them. They had expected them to return and were now getting worried. As they swam around calling out the girls' names, they heard a reply and discovered it was coming from the locked cell. Ariel and Rosy were delighted to see that the twins were safe and tried to reach out to them through the tiny window in the door. Their relief soon turned to concern, though: the monster fish would be back soon and might lock the babies up, too! They had to get them away from there!

Ariel's face fell as she saw one of the younger fish swimming over to the twins. The fish grabbed hold of the twins and squealed with delight. She thought the babies looked like fun and wanted to take them home to play with - she had always wanted some living dolls! Her father agreed that she could keep them, then turned sternly to the mermaids and ordered that they do some cleaning. He still hadn't decided what he should do with them, but thought they may as well do something useful while he was thinking about it.

The tears welled in Rosy's eyes as she obediently swept the floor. What had at first seemed like an adventure was now turning into a nightmare. She wondered if her baby cousins were still all right, then began to worry about what her poor aunt would do if they didn't return home soon. As Ariel crossly prodded her broom around, she thought and thought of a way to get them out of this mess and away from those monsters. She had no idea that not far away, the mischievous twins were up to their usual tricks...

Excited by having somewhere new to play, the babies were causing havoc in the young fish's house. They chased small fish, then chased each other, and broke every toy that they played with. In desperation, the fat little fish called for her parents to come and do something. The grown-ups stared aghast at the babies as they hared round the room, crashing into furniture. They tried shouting at them to stop, but it was no use. The twins were enjoying themselves far too much to listen to some bloated old fish telling them what to do! They dashed around giggling,

then swam close to the fish, giving the father a playful thump and a bite as they passed.

The mother fish knew who could help and swam off to see Ariel. Seeing her chance, the little mermaid demanded freedom in exchange for getting the babies under control again. The fish readily agreed - they would have given anything to get rid of those dreadful babies! They watched with relief as the twins swam away to greet Ariel and Rosy.

Ariel and Rosy each cuddled a twin and turned to go, as the bewildered fish stared after them. The twins smiled and sucked their thumbs innocently. Even so, Ariel warned Rosy not to let go of her twin until they were safely back home: she'd had quite enough for one day and didn't want any more trouble! Rosy, now confident in the knowledge that they would soon be back at her aunt's, felt quite excited as she thought about the adventure they'd just had. She couldn't wait to tell her friends back home about the strange creatures of the abyss!

The mermaids and the twins were all relieved to swim back into the bright, clear waters of the kingdom. Back at the palace, the girls returned the twins to their mother just as she had finished all the jobs she had to do. She smiled down at her contented babies and asked how they had been. In her desperation to keep the twins' escape a secret, Rosy ended up agreeing to look after the babies for the next two days. As Ariel shot her a surprised glance, she shrugged her shoulders. It might not be too bad, and they might even have another big adventure!

Treasure Trove

Ariel is always searching ship wrecks for new 'human treasures' to add to her collection. If you take the first letter of each object below, you can rearrange the letters to spell out the name of one of Ariel's sea friends! The answer is at the bottom of the page.

Marine Maze

Uh-oh! Ariel and Flounder are in trouble! Help Spot the whale swim through the maze to save them before the shark swallows them whole!

SCHOOL'S OUT

Hooray! School's out for summer for Max, so it's down with the text books and up with the comics! Can you unjumble the letters to work out which school books Max has thrown away until next term? The answers are at the bottom of the page.

GPRAOYHEG

SPINAHS

LGOBYIO

TRYSHIO

HISCTEMATAM

CEICENS

56

GONE FISHING

Uh-oh! Goofy thought it would be a great idea to go on a fishing trip, but it isn't Max's idea of fun! Follow the fishing lines to find out who's caught dinner! The answer is at the bottom of the page.

57

Answer: Max has caught the whopper!

LETTERS OF LOVE

Max is in lurve! He's missing Roxanne while on holiday and has decided to write some notes to her. He's had to write them in code, though, so his dad can't read them. One note is a mirror image, another has numbers corresponding to the alphabet (A=1, B=2 etc.). Have a peek and see what he's saying! The answers are at the bottom of the page.

Answers: Note 1: Dear Roxanne. This fishing trip is so boring! I wish I was back home with you instead of stuck here with my Dad! See you soon. Love, Max.
Note 2: Dear Roxanne, Sorry I couldn't come to the party. I'll make it up to you. Love, I promise! Max.

WHAT A FALL!

Whoah! Now things are getting a little more lively! Goofy and Max are trying some water sports, but they've lost their luggage along the way. Can you spot 5 of their lost belongings in the picture? The answers are at the bottom of the page.

Answers: binoculars, camera, suitcase, frying pan, football.

RUNAWAY BRAIN

MICKEY MOUSE

When Mickey forgets the anniversary of his first date with Minnie, he's in trouble! Unwittingly promising her a dream holiday in Hawaii, he finds a way of earning the money for it - but ends up being part of a terrifying brain-swapping experiment!

JULIUS

This huge, fierce monster is Dr. Frankenollie's manufactured helper. When his brain is transferred to Mickey's body, he becomes obsessed with Minnie and begins a hair-raising chase across the city after spotting her in a boutique.

MINNIE MOUSE

Mickey's long-time girlfriend dotes on him, but does get mad occasionally, especially when he pays more attention to his computer games than he does to her! Minnie can be tough, too - no monster can kidnap her without a fight!

PLUTO

Pluto the dog is Mickey's faithful friend and constant companion. Seeing his master in trouble, he does his best to help by solving Mickey's money problem - or so he thinks!

It was a stormy afternoon and thunder ripped through the air as sharp needles of rain poured down from heavy, black clouds. Inside, Mickey was absorbed in his latest computer game. He shouted excitedly at the screen as he zapped, making Pluto bark and leap around the furniture.

Mickey was so engrossed in his game, he didn't hear Minnie calling him as she came into the house. "I'm really looking forward to tonight!" she smiled. Mickey still ignored her. "I said, I'm so excited about tonight!" she went on, standing in front of the screen. Diving to one side, Mickey banged the joystick, just saving his game life! Minnie sighed. It was obvious Mickey had forgotten the anniversary of their very first date. He tried to deny it, but it was too late. Minnie stormed towards the door.

Then Mickey spotted a newspaper advertisement showing a 'two for one' miniature golfing holiday. What a stroke of luck! He could go golfing and pretend he'd planned it as a special trip for them both!

Mickey laughed and proudly held up the newspaper, declaring that he'd had the anniversary celebration planned all along. Minnie wasn't convinced at first, but softened when she heard the magic word 'sun'. She took the paper from Mickey's hand and was delighted to see an advertisement for a dream holiday in Hawaii! Giving Mickey a big hug, she planted a kiss on his lips.

Before Mickey could explain to Minnie that she had read the wrong advertisement, she rushed out of the door to go on a special shopping trip. A holiday wasn't a holiday without new clothes!

"Oh, well, if it makes Minnie happy, then it's worth paying ... nine hundred and ninety nine pounds?" gasped Mickey. "Pluto, I don't have nine hundred and ninety nine pence! What am I gonna do?"

As Mickey paced the room, Pluto showed him the 'want' ads. Puzzled, Mickey looked through them until he finally saw what Pluto was looking at.

Mickey smiled. There in the ads was the perfect solution to his problem. He could get all the money he needed for the holiday from just one day's work, and an easy day's work at that! Mickey gave Pluto an affectionat rub on the head and thanked him. What a clever dog!

It was getting late, but Mickey didn't want anyone else to get the job first. Leaving Pluto in the warm, he set off through the dark, wet streets. At last, he stood in front of an imposing old mansion.

"This is it! 1313 Lobotomy Lane!" grinned Mickey, reading out the marble wall plaque and checking the address with the ad.

Snapping on a clip-on tie, Mickey banged the door-knocker and waited for an answer. The door didn't open, but the pavement did! "YEAOOOOW!" screamed Mickey, falling through a trap-door into a long chute. With a thunk, he landed in a chair inside a laboratory.

Steel clamps quickly locked over Mickey's hands, legs and body.

"I knew this was too good to be true!" he muttered, as a figure swung in front of him.

"Dr. Frankenollie at your service!" grinned an ape. "So you want the job, huh?"

"I w-was, but I think I've changed my m-mind!" stammered Mickey.

"Changed you mind?" cackled the doctor. "Well, that may turn out to be truer than you imagine!"

The doctor pressed a button on a remote control device and the floor opened, revealing a fierce-looking monster.

"Wait a minute! What's going on?" gasped Mickey, getting more nervous by the second. The doctor explained that the monster was his own creation and that Mickey was lucky enough to be working with him. Mickey shrank back in his seat as the roaring creature seemed to grow enormous. Swinging over Mickey's head, the ape sprang forward and plugged in a monitor.

A series of x-rays appeared on the screen, revealing Mickey's brain, and the doctor became even more excited! He told the monster, whose name was Julius, that he had found him a new brain. Mickey was astounded to learn that the doctor's plan was to swap his brain with the monster's!

As Doctor Frankenollie threw a switch, bolts of electricity lit the room. Bouncing off walls, the current shot through the air in different directions. His mad laughter still ringing in the air, bolts of electricity struck the doctor first. As Mickey began to fry in his chair, Doctor Frankenollie exploded, leaving a swirling trail of smoke!

The sparking and fizzing gradually died down until there was silence in the laboratory. Mickey and Julius both groaned as they began to recover from their ordeal. They peered groggily through the smoke to try and discover what had happened.

As the smoke cleared, Mickey whispered, "Ooh, I don't feel like myself! I..."

Looking down at his body, Mickey realised what had happened. "I-I'm not myself!" he gulped. Mickey's brain was now inside the monster's body!

As Doctor Frankenollie's body disintegrated into a pile of ashes, the monster, in Mickey's body, jumped out of the debris. Looking down at the roaring 'monster',

Mickey tried to soothe him, telling him to look at the photos in his wallet to see who he was. As the monster opened the wallet, several photos dropped out. Mickey pointed Minnie out to him.

"And she likes my body and my mind, both in the same place!" he added.

Mickey tried to take back his wallet, but the little monster went berserk! He had obviously taken a liking to the pretty mouse in the photograph.

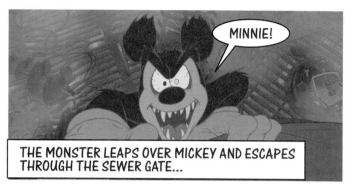

THE MONSTER LEAPS OVER MICKEY AND ESCAPES THROUGH THE SEWER GATE...

STOP! THIEF! COME BACK WITH MY BODY!

THE MONSTER TAKES NO NOTICE...

...AND CLIMBS OUT ON TO THE ROOF.

DOWN IN THE STREET, MINNIE IS GOING SHOPPING FOR HOLIDAY CLOTHES...

...AND SHE'S BEEN SPOTTED!

WHOAH! MINNIE!

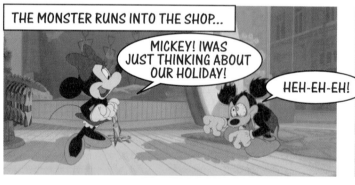

THE MONSTER RUNS INTO THE SHOP...

MICKEY! I WAS JUST THINKING ABOUT OUR HOLIDAY!

HEH-EH-EH!

AH, AH, AH! NOT TILL WE'RE ON THE BOAT!

Lunging at Mickey, the monster crawled up his body, saying Minnie's name over and over again. He catapulted over the top of Mickey's head and escaped from the laboratory.
"Where are you going with my body? We gotta switch brains!" called Mickey, desparately.

Peering over the laboratory roof, the monster saw Minnie going into a shop down below.
"Minnie...Minnie!" he roared.

"So many styles and so little time," grinned Minnie, taking a tiny green bikini down from a rack inside the shop. Holding it up, she wondered whether Mickey would like it. She smiled as she thought about the wonderful holiday they were going to have together.

Suddenly, the monster burst through the door. Minnie smiled. She thought it was Mickey and was pleased to see him! She noticed the strange look in his eyes, but put it down to pre-holiday excitement.

Just at that moment, Mickey crashed through the shop window and grabbed the monster away from Minnie. "I didn't think I'd get here in time!" gasped Mickey with relief, looking down from the monster's body. But Minnie didn't recognise the monster's voice.

"Leave me alone!" she cried.

Throwing anything she could get her hands on, Minnie rmanaged to set the monster free. She grabbed his hand and dragged him from the shop. Crashing through the

storefront, Mickey used a bus to chase after the pair, quickly catching up with them. He scooped Minnie up into his enormous hands and tried to reassure her.

"Let go of me, you, you MONSTER!" screeched Minnie, not listening to what he was saying.

Before he knew what was happening, Minnie punched Mickey on the nose - again and again! He struggled to keep a grip on her as she wriggled furiously and kicked at his fingers, yelling for help.

Rubbing his nose, Mickey gasped, "Minnie, stop! It's me! Mickey!" Minnie stopped screaming and spluttered. She could tell it really was Mickey, but what had happened to him?

Suddenly, they heard again the roar of the monster. He was approaching on the bonnet of a speeding car. Leaping off the bus, Mickey used a crane to swing to the top of a building. Leaving Minnie on the roof-top, he swung away to fight with the monster.

As the monster turned to run, Mickey swooped down and grabbed his tail, cheered on by Minnie. "Got you this time, buster!" grinned Mickey, as the monster waved his arms in the air.

Mickey had spoken too soon! Pulling on the bucket, the monster released some bricks, knocking Mickey from the crane. Mickey tried to hold on to the monster, but it was no good. They both slipped further and further, until the monster's grip loosened.

THE PAIR HAVE FALLEN ON TO POWER LINES AND THEIR BRAINS GLOW IN THE ELECTRIC SURGE.

BZZZTTTZZZ!

CRACKLE!

THEY ARE CATAPULTED INTO THE AIR...

AAAARGH!

...AND LAND IN A HUGE BILLBOARD.

ARE YOU ALL RIGHT?

BUT THE MONSTER HAS HIS BRAIN BACK!

UH-OH!

RRAAAAAGH!

THE MONSTER HAS MINNIE IN ONE HAND AND MICKEY IN THE OTHER.

YAHAHAAAR!

THEN...

WAAAH!

HELP!

AAAAAARGH!

Falling from the crane, the monster and Mickey fell on to power lines, causing an electric surge. Their brains glowing, the pair catapulted into the air - heading back towards the top of the building!

Sweeping up Minnie in his hand, the monster crashed through a huge billboard.
"Minnie! Wh-What's going on?" gasped Mickey, now back inside his own body.
"Mickey? Mickey! Oh, my! You're you again! Things are getting stranger by the minute!" gasped Minnie.

Smacking his lips, the monster laughed as he held on to Minnie.
"Hey, let her go, you fiend!" called Mickey.
Roaring in Mickey's face, the monster broke out of the billboard. Mickey wasn't giving up! Opening his mouth wide, he bit the monster's hand.
"Yearghhhhh!" cried the monster, flicking Mickey over the side of the building.

71

MICKEY HAS BEEN TOSSED ASIDE...

OH, NO! MICKEY!

...BUT NOT FOR LONG!

HEY, YOU! JULIUS!

WAAAAAH!

YAAAAAAH!

MICKEY CHARGES TOWARDS JULIUS.

JULIUS TRIES TO STOP HIM, BUT MISSES!

MICKEY POLE VAULTS OVER THE MONSTER...

...AND TIES ONE END OF HIS LASSO TO THE BILLBOARD.

Mickey went spinning through the air as Minnie looked on helplessly. The monster cackled, but the action wasn't over yet. Mickey had landed on a window cleaner's platform. He rose up the side of the building and reappeared. He was ready for the final confrontation!

Clutching a long-handled squeegee, Mickey held it aloft and began to charge at the monster. "Now let's see what you're really made of, Julius!" he cried, as he gathered up speed.

Pole-vaulting over the monster, Mickey landed on the billboard. Lassoing one end of his rope to the moving arm of a hula girl, Mickey bravely leaped at the monster. "It's not the size of your body that counts when it comes to winning! It's the size of your brain!" called Mickey. "And your brain's the size of a pea, Julius!"

The monster roared in frustration as Mickey dodged his grasp time and again. His huge, clumsy hands were no match for this agile little mouse.

MICKEY SWINGS BACK TO THE ROOF...

...MAKING JULIUS DROP MINNIE OVER THE EDGE!

AAAIIEEEEE!

DON'T WORRY, MINNIE! I GOTCHA!

MICKEY PUTS HIS LASSO TO GOOD USE!

OH, MICKEY! THAT WAS CLOSE!

IT'S ALL OKAY NOW.

WHILE THE COUPLE ARE REUNITED, JULIUS TEETERS OVER THE EDGE!

AAAAAAAARGH!

SOME TIME LATER...

HAPPY ANNIVERSARY, MINNIE.

MINNIE! MINNIE!

SMACK!

THE END

As Mickey tied up the monster, Minnie fell screaming over the edge of the building. Holding on to the rope, Mickey swung to the rescue, plucking Minnie out of the air.

Safely back on the roof, Minnie gave Mickey a 'monster'-sized hug! As the pair stood beneath the smashed Hawaii billboard, the monster teetered on the edge of the roof.
"Our holiday is ruined - just like this billboard!" sighed

Minnie. Suddenly, he monster lost his balance and toppled over the edge! Still tied to the rope and the hula dancer, he boinged up and down like a yo-yo!
"I have an idea..." grinned Mickey.

Mickey wished Minnie a Happy Anniversary, as they drifted through the South Pacific waters.
"You're sooo romantic," whispered Minnie. And the monster? He swam towards Hawaii, pulling the love-birds on a raft, still calling Minnie's name!

73

THE GARGOYLES

The gargoyles, Hugo, Victor and Laverne, are Quasimodo's close friends and are always ready to give him advice - whether he wants it or not!

PHOEBUS

Phoebus was ordered to deal with the capital's gypsies, but his task was made impossible when he fell in love with Esmeralda, a beautiful gypsy girl.

DJALI

Djali is Esmeralda's companion. He is always ready to give a well-aimed butt if the pair are moved on whilst performing.

FROLLO

Judge Frollo is Quasimodo's master. He killed Quasimodo's mother when the boy was a baby, so as punishment, the Archdeacon of Paris ordered Frollo to care for the child and raise him as his own son.

ESMERALDA AND QUASIMODO

Quasimodo is the bell-ringer of Notre Dame. Esmeralda, the strong-willed gypsy girl, defied the Festival crowds and Frollo when she showed Quasimodo the kindness that began their close friendship.

IT'S SPRINGTIME IN PARIS! THERE ARE SIGNS OF NEW LIFE EVERYWHERE, EVEN IN THE BELL TOWER WHERE QUASIMODO LIVES...

It was a beautiful spring afternoon in Paris. Notre Dame, the city's huge cathedral, basked in warm sunshine as a flock of chirruping birds circled its tower before settling on the city roofs below. The surrounding streets were bustling with cheerful townspeople who were making the most of the nice weather and looking forward to the coming summer. There was one Parisian, however, who could only enjoy the sunshine from his small balcony. His name was Quasimodo and he lived in the cathedral's bell tower...

WITH A FACE LIKE THIS, HOW COULD ANYONE EVER LIKE ME?

CHIRP! CHIRP!

THUMP!

WHAT'S ALL THAT NOISE?

Quasimodo had spent his whole life in the tower of Notre Dame. For as long as he could remember, his master, the evil Judge Frollo, had forbidden him to ever leave the cathedral. Frollo had told Quasimodo that he was ugly and deformed and the people of the city would be cruel to him. The bell ringer often brooded on his misfortune, looking into his mirror daily and agonising over his hideous features. He asked himself time and again how anyone could ever grow to love him when he looked the way he did. Esmeralda, the beautiful gypsy girl, had

been very kind to him, but he knew she could never love him. He believed his master when he told him he could never be like normal people.

That spring afternoon, Quasimodo's thoughts were interrupted by a strange noise outside. Putting his mirror back on the table, he went on to the balcony and asked his friends, the three gargoyles, what was going on. Seeing that Laverne was cradling something in her hands, he looked more closely to see what it was.

In the middle of Laverne's grey palm sat a dazed baby bird. She held him out to Quasimodo, explaining that the noise had been him crashing into the balcony. He had then fallen on to the floor and broken his leg. Quasimodo peered closer and gasped when he saw the bird's bent limb. It looked very painful. The little bird didn't seem to mind too much, though. He introduced himself, telling everyone that his name was Charlie and that he had hurt himself whilst trying to fly. He became a little more upset when he discovered that his parents had continued on their journey

without him. He would never be able to catch up with them now!

Quasimodo and the gargoyles were worried about the chick and knew they would have to help him to get better. Laverne examined Charlie's tiny leg again, while he looked on curiously, occasionally glancing up at her expectantly. After prodding the leg gently and wiggling Charlie's toes for a few moments, Laverne declared that the injury was serious and needed immediate attention.

Quasimodo smiled down at Charlie and told him not to worry. He knew exactly what to do! They all went back into the tower and Laverne gently lay the injured chick down on the table. They all gathered round as Quasimodo lit a ceiling lamp and rubbed his hands, as if about to take on a challenging task. Charlie propped himself up with one wing and watched with interest as Quasimodo played the part of the doctor, whilst Laverne was the nurse, passing along all the things necessary to bandage up the little broken leg. Victor and Hugo winced now and then as they watched the operation from the end of the table, sharing in Charlie's pain.

Finally, Quasimodo was finished. He helped Charlie to his feet and proudly admired his work. The brave little bird wobbled on his good leg for a moment, then got his balance and looked down at the bandage. He gasped. It was huge, and it felt so heavy! He could hardly move, let alone walk. He didn't think he'd ever get used to getting around with all that weight on his leg.

Quasimodo assured Charlie that it wouldn't be long before they could take the bandages off and he could try flying again. In the meantime, though, he would have to put up with looking like a mummy. The chick still wasn't satisfied. Even with the bandages on, he could tell that his leg was so badly broken, it would be crooked forever. He dreaded the thought of being the butt of all the other birds' jokes. Laverne smiled. She was certain that this lively little bird could easily get through life with a bent leg!

Finally, the time came to remove Charlie's bandage. Quasimodo unwrapped it carefully, then pulled it right off and stood back. He was delighted to see that the leg had mended very well, all thanks to him! Charlie, on the other hand, was disappointed to have his fears confirmed as he looked down at his damaged limb: his leg was far from normal. It looked even worse when he put it next to his good leg. He was more sure than ever that the other birds would make fun of him. The thought of being laughed at for the rest of his life filled him with dread.

Quasimodo and Laverne did their best to comfort Charlie, but whatever they said didn't seem to be enough. The little bird was very self-conscious of his leg and worried about it constantly, brooding on what the other birds would think of him. The days and weeks went by and Charlie got stronger, until Quasimodo thought the time was right for him to try and fly again. Still lacking in confidence, Charlie insisted that he wouldn't be able to do it, but agreed to try all the same to please Quasimodo. Jumping from his friend's finger, he was astounded to find

that it wasn't as difficult as he thought it would be. He could fly! Quasimodo had been right all along!

Desperate to show off his new skill, Charlie flew out to the balcony and chirruped excitedly at Laverne. She chuckled and clapped as she watched him fly round in circles, calling out words of encouragement. It was only when she mentioned his leaving that Charlie became a little afraid, glancing nervously at the city below. He decided he'd flown far enough for one day.

The last of Charlie's excitement evaporated as he landed on Laverne's hand and held up his crooked leg. He began to worry again about mixing with the other birds. How could he possibly join them again, looking the way he did? He'd probably scare them off! Laverne gazed at Charlie and frowned a little. It was only natural that any young bird would be worried about his appearance, but Charlie had become obsessed by it. She thought for a moment, then began to smile as she realised why he was so worried. He was just being a boy. Charlie then shyly

admitted that it was finding a mate that was making him so anxious!

The gargoyles and Quasimodo all looked affectionately at Charlie. He was such a lively little bird. They knew there would be plenty of female birds out there who would fall in love with him! All they had to do was convince him. Quasimodo pointed out that Charlie hadn't been put off by his appearance and didn't mind being his friend, despite what Frollo said.

Quasimodo insisted that looks didn't matter and that what really counted was personality. He secretly wished he could believe it himself! Finally reassured, Charlie thanked his friends for their kindness and said farewell as he sprung from Quasimodo's hand. As they watched him fly off into the distance, Quasimodo and the gargoyles waved and shouted to their little friend until he had disappeared from view into the clouds. They were sad to see him go. It had made quite a change to have a youngster around the place!

A hot summer followed that warm spring and Quasimodo and the gargoyles carried on with their lives as usual, protected from the heat by the cool shade of the tower. From time to time, one of them would mention Charlie and they would all wonder where he was and what he was doing.

Leaves then began to fall from the trees as the seasons changed again, bringing chilly winds that whistled round the cathedral and sent draughts through the tower.

Of all the gargoyles, Hugo most hated the colder seasons. It seemed that he was constantly shivering from autumn until spring! He especially disliked the snowy weather, particularly when he had to sit outside with the icy flakes gathering on his shoulders. He couldn't understand why the children of the town played in the stuff in the streets below - they even picked it up in their hands and threw it at one another! Laverne would often get fed up with Hugo's moaning. She was a tough old gargoyle and couldn't see what all the fuss was about.

The months soon passed and another spring arrived. The city's trees were heavy with fresh, green leaves again, the sun was warm and the sound of birds echoed round the cathedral once more. Hugo still wasn't happy, though. He insisted that the spring flowers brought on his hay fever! Quasimodo smiled. He loved to see the city bursting with colour again and enjoyed breathing in the fresh, spring air first thing in the morning. The scent of flowers was his favourite smell and he even had his own small garden to care for.

Quasimodo tended to his pots of flowers as Hugo looked on with admiration. The little gargoyle agreed that the flowers were beautiful, but pointed out that there were weeds amongst them and suggested that they should be pulled out. As he poured a jug of water on his little garden, Quasimodo disagreed, pointing out that many weeds were just as pretty as flowers. He was startled to hear a familiar voice agreeing with him from the balcony ledge. He glanced up to check that he wasn't mistaken, and smiled. It was Charlie!

Charlie had come back to see his friends at Notre Dame; he hadn't forgotten the kindness they'd shown him the previous spring when he was so badly injured on their balcony. Quasimodo and the gargoyles were delighted to see him again and greeted him warmly. He still had a crooked leg, of course, but he had grown up into a fine, strong bird. Suddenly, there was a strange sound behind him. Quasimodo looked puzzled - he thought he was hearing things. It was exactly the sound he'd heard on that spring day a year ago!

Charlie stepped aside and the others gasped as they saw two baby birds standing beside him. The pair had managed to safely crash-land on to the balcony ledge and stood grinning at their audience. They looked just like Charlie used to when he was small - except without the crooked leg, of course! Charlie proudly announced that these were his two sons and their names were Peter and Jack. He was then joined by another bird, a female who landed gracefully beside him on the ledge. Charlie introduced her as his wife, Marie.

Quasimodo and the gargoyles welcomed Charlie's family. They always knew he would have no trouble finding a mate, and now he had two sons as well! Putting his wing round Marie's shoulders, Charlie smiled at Quasimodo and agreed that all he had told him had been true; his leg hadn't made much difference to his life at all. Marie pointed out that it had, in fact, made him stand out from the crowd as something special - it was his strength in dealing with the problem that had impressed her so much. Charlie smiled at her affectionately.

Charlie and his family sat at the bell-tower for some time, chatting happily away to Quasimodo, but their visit was soon over. They had a long journey to the coast ahead of them and had to get going before it became too dark. They promised to return soon and said their goodbyes. Quasimodo and the gargoyles waved them off as they flew into the sunset.

Quasimodo turned to go back into the bell-tower, still thinking about the surprise visit. He was so pleased that Charlie had found the happiness he thought he'd never have. As he passed the table, he noticed the mirror and picked it up thoughtfully. Gazing at his reflection, he felt hope for the first time. Perhaps the day would come when he would be as happy as Charlie, when someone accepted him for who he was and not what he looked like.

Suddenly, it dawned on Quasimodo that he could see something in the mirror that he had never seen before - his own smile!

Fancy Dress

It's the Festival of Fools and everyone is going to wear fancy dress. The pieces of clothing below make up 4 complete outfits. Help Clopin to match them all up! The answers are at the bottom of the page.

Spot The Difference

These two pictures of Quasimodo's gargoyle friends look the same, but there are ten differences between them. Can you spot them all? The answers are at the bottom of the page.

Answers: The curtain is missing, the large flying bird has moved, the other flying bird is missing, a bird has gone from Victor's hand, Hugo's left arm has moved, the building in the background is missing, the pot on the ledge is missing, Laverne's left arm has moved, the stool is missing, the yellow cloth on the ledge is different.

Festival Of Fools

Everyone's cheering Esmeralda as she dances at the Festival of Fools. Look carefully at the picture, then see if you can answer the following questions. The answers are at the bottom of the page.

Many people in the crowd are throwing their hats in the air as they cheer. How many flying hats can you count altogether?

How many banners are there amongst the crowd? Which two banners are the same?

A festival wouldn't be a festival without music! There are 3 musical instruments in the picture - what are they?

Answers: There are nine flying hats; there are five banners; the banners at the far right and far left are the same; there are 3 instruments: a tambourine, a flute and a violin.

101 Dalmatians

The Dalmatian Puppies

Here are just three of the fifteen Dalmatian puppies that are about to celebrate their birthday. Like any puppies, they spend most of their time bounding around and causing mischief - when they're not watching television, of course!

Thunderbolt

This brave hound is every dog's hero, especially Lucky's! He's universally famous for his Wild West TV adventures, but his stardom doesn't stop him giving the Dalmatian puppies a birthday trip to remember.

Lucky

This little puppy is Thunderbolt's biggest fan. He admires the TV dog so much that he even dreams about him! He has no idea that he will have his own five minutes of fame on his birthday, when he himself becomes the hero!

Pongo and Perdita

These two grown-up Dalmatians are mother and father to Lucky and the other puppies. The doting parents want only the best for their puppies and are delighted when Thunderbolt agrees to be involved in their special birthday treat.

92

Pongo and Perdita were Dalmatians. They lived in a beautiful big house in London with their litter of fifteen puppies and, of course, their owners, Roger and Anita. The puppies were always bursting with energy and from the moment they woke up in the mornings, they would run excitedly round the house. Roger and Anita had to make sure that they took their dogs out for a walk every day - the puppies especially enjoyed trips to the park, where they had plenty of room to leap about in.

Anyone would think that after a hard day's playing, the Dalmatian puppies would be ready for bed. Nothing could be further from the truth! Every evening, they loved to watch Thunderbolt on television and stay up as late as they could to follow their hero's adventures. Each puppy would scamper around the living room until he had chosen a comfortable spot and settle down to stare up avidly at the brave dog on screen. It was the only time all the puppies sat still - or at least, almost all of them...

One evening, the puppies were all watching their favourite programme as usual, when suddenly they all started yelping crossly. One of the puppies, Lucky, had got so excited at Thunderbolt's story that he had run up to the television to talk to him! He stood up against the screen and pressed his nose to it, shouting words of encouragement at his hero, to help him escape from the villain. The other puppies didn't think it was such a good idea, though. They couldn't see the television screen! They all shouted at him to move out of the way, so they wouldn't miss any more of the show. They were just as eager to see what happened to Thunderbolt as Lucky was!

Pongo and Perdita heard all the noise from the next room and came in to try and calm their children down. It was something they had become quite used to doing! Smiling at the puppies, they decided it was time for them all to go to bed, whether they liked it or not!

Whilst most of the puppies objected to being sent to bed, some were already falling asleep on their feet. As always, it took Pongo quite some time to round them all up - they would watch Thunderbolt's adventures all night if they could! They tried all sorts of tricks to put off the bedtime routine, but Pongo was wise to their ways and always managed to win in the end. He chased and pushed, and nudged and pulled, until all the puppies were out of the living room. Now all he had to do was get them into their baskets and persuade them to stay there!

Pongo hadn't noticed, though, that he was missing a pup! Lucky had sneaked back into the living room and bounded over to the television to see a few more minutes of his favourite programme. He snuggled down on the soft carpet in front of the screen and began to watch again, but it wasn't long before his eyelids began to droop. He changed position and tried to open his eyes wide, but it was no good. All that playing earlier was beginning to catch up with him. It seemed that the harder he tried to keep his tired eyes open, the drowsier he became...

Lucky stretched himself out on the floor and quickly drifted off into a deep sleep. His eyes and legs twitched as he began to dream about Thunderbolt being chased by the villain again. He felt as if he was right there in the desert, watching the action! Suddenly, he saw that poor Thunderbolt's escape path was blocked by rocks. He was trapped! The brave dog turned to face the crook and snarled at him to keep away, his star badge glinting in the hot sun. The villain only sneered and came closer, reaching for his gun.

Suddenly, Lucky bounded across to Thunderbolt and stood between him and the crook, yelping furiously. He was going to protect his hero, no matter what! The least he could do was to distract the man from pointing his gun at them. The fat cowboy crossed his arms and sniggered maliciously. What could a little spotty puppy do to harm him? Lucky didn't like being scoffed at and soon showed what he could do. He sped between the villain's legs, sending him off balance and taking his attention away from Thunderbolt...

The cowboy gasped and waved his arms about in an attempt to regain his balance, but Lucky scampered back towards him. The brave little puppy lunged at the meaty leg before him and took a huge bite from the villain's trousers, before running away again. The man cried out in surprise and toppled over into the dust with a loud thump.

Panting angrily and rubbing his leg, the cowboy got up and glared at Lucky. He strode towards him, bellowing with rage. Lucky was a little afraid now and backed away towards Thunderbolt for help. Whimpering slightly, he wondered if this time he had bitten off more than he could chew!

Thunderbolt crept closer to Lucky and looked warily up at the villain, trying desperately to think of a plan. He had been in worse situations than this before and had always managed to escape. This time, though, he had a young friend to protect, too.

A loud, low growl suddenly stopped everyone in their tracks. The huge shadow of a dog fell upon the rocks nearby and everyone gasped. Lucky ran over to the shadow and jumped up against it, puzzled. Where was it coming from? The cowboy gulped as the growling voice snarled a warning to him. It was the legendary Great Coyote! Beginning to sweat with fear, he backed away slowly. After stuttering a warning to Thunderbolt that he would get him next time, he scuttled off into the distance. Lucky took a look at the Great Coyote that had scared

away the nasty cowboy. It was his dad! His dad had rescued him and Thunderbolt, the boldest dog in the West! How brave he was!

P ongo smiled at his dreaming son and nudged him gently to try and wake him up. He was sleeping very soundly. Thunderbolt's show had finished some time before, but even the buzzing television had not woken him up. Pongo picked Lucky up by his collar and carried him off to bed to join his brothers and sisters.

A week or so later, it was the puppies' birthday. It wasn't always easy for Pongo and Perdita to think of birthday treats for their fifteen children, but this year they had thought of the perfect surprise. They rounded the puppies up and set off on a long walk.

A ll the way there, the puppies yelped and bounced around excitedly, demanding to know where they were going. Even when they reached a huge park, they still couldn't guess what lay in store. They nagged and nagged at their parents to tell them where they were going, but Pongo and Perdita refused to give in. The puppies' birthday surprise was to remain a surprise!

The dogs walked along one path after another through the green park, becoming more and more curious about their treat. The puppies ran to and fro, looking around for any clues, then giving up and pestering their parents again. Pongo and Perdita would only smile and tell their children to wait and see.

Finally, Pongo stopped in the middle of the park. He turned to the puppies and announced that they had arrived! The puppies all stood still, bewildered. Where was their birthday surprise? All they could see was another group of dogs in the distance. It wasn't anyone they knew...was it?

It didn't take long for Lucky to recognise the dog in the middle of the nearby group. It was Thunderbolt! The puppies all gasped in awe and were silent for a moment.

They'd only ever seen Thunderbolt on the television screen, and now there he was: right in front of them! All at once, the puppies broke into a run and sped, cheering, towards their hero.

Thunderbolt looked up from the group of fans surrounding him and smiled. All those little spotty dogs running down the hill towards him were quite a sight! They all bumped into one another as they slid to a stop in front of him and stared.

It was obvious that the film star had been expecting the Dalmatians. What's more, he knew it was their birthday. The puppies were astounded! How on earth did he know? Was he so special that he could remember the birthday of every puppy in the world? It took a few moments for them to realise that this was their birthday present: Pongo and Perdita had made special arrangements for them to meet their hero. The puppies all laughed and thanked their mum and dad. What a brilliant idea they'd come up with this year! It had to be the best present ever!

Thunderbolt had been looking forward to meeting the puppies. He enjoyed meeting all his fans, but he especially liked to talk to the younger ones. He had been told that of all the puppies, Lucky was his biggest fan, and looked out for him. Although the young Dalmatians were all delighted to be only yards from their hero, they stayed close to their parents. Only Lucky had the courage to go bounding up to speak to him. Thunderbolt gave his paw a hearty shake and welcomed him to the park, where he would soon be filming more of his adventures.

Lucky was delighted to find that Thunderbolt already knew his name and had been told all about him. He proudly walked beside his hero as they began to wander along the river, chatting as they went. He could hardly believe he was going for a casual stroll with the famous star! All of a sudden, Thunderbolt seemed to lose his footing on the grass and went tumbling down the bank into the river. He landed flat on his back in the water with a huge splash and cried out for help as his arms and legs flailed helplessly.

Lucky didn't waste a moment: Thunderbolt needed rescuing, just as he did in the dream the week before. It was almost as if the dream had been a warning! The bold little puppy leaped into the river after Thunderbolt and dived under the water. He soon surfaced with Thunderbolt's famous star collar between his teeth and helped the dog swim back towards the riverbank.Lucky's brothers and sisters stood at the front of the crowd that had gathered to see what was going on and watched in awe as he came closer.

The puppies helped Thunderbolt and Lucky back on to dry land. They could hardly believe what they had seen. Their own brother had rescued the world famous Thunderbolt! It was just like an episode of the show - what a thrilling birthday this had turned out to be! The film star congratulated Pongo and Perdita on their son's bravery. Lucky grinned proudly and shook the water from his coat, while all the other puppies looked at each other in wonder. None of them noticed Pongo and Thunderbolt exchange knowing winks...

Perdita and Pongo were so pleased that the puppies had enjoyed their birthday. It had taken a lot of organising, but had all been worth the trouble. They were very grateful to Thunderbolt for thinking of such spectacular entertainment for the afternoon!

Unfortunately, Thunderbolt had work to do. He was, after all, a famous star on a film set and was being called by his crew to start shooting again. It seemed that he would soon have to leave them.

Thunderbolt, however, said that the film crew would have to wait for the time being. He wasn't going to work when he had a birthday party to go to! Lucky and his brothers and sisters stared up at him in disbelief. Not only had they met their favourite star, now he was coming home with them, too! As all the dogs made their way back through the park, the puppies scampered ahead to show Thunderbolt the way to their house, while he walked between Pongo and Perdita, chatting as he went. He was just a normal dog, really!

Once home, the dogs all rushed into the living room to start the party games. They had lots of fun, especially when Thunderbolt joined in and taught them some of his favourite games!

Later, the grown-ups sang Happy Birthday for the children, before giving them slices of birthday cake. Lucky automatically went to turn the television on, then realised that he didn't have to - Thunderbolt was already in the room, having cake with them! What a birthday!

Birthday Treats

Lucky loves birthday teas - look at all the fairy cakes he has to choose from! If you match all the pairs, there is one cake left over. Which cake is the odd one out? The answer is at the bottom of the page.

Answer: H is the odd cake out.

Time For Bed

Those Dalmatian puppies never want to go to bed, even if they're not watching Thunderbolt on the television! There should be 15 puppies altogether in the room. How many puppies have escaped from Nanny? The answer is at the bottom of the page.

Answer: There are 13 puppies in the picture, so two puppies have escaped!

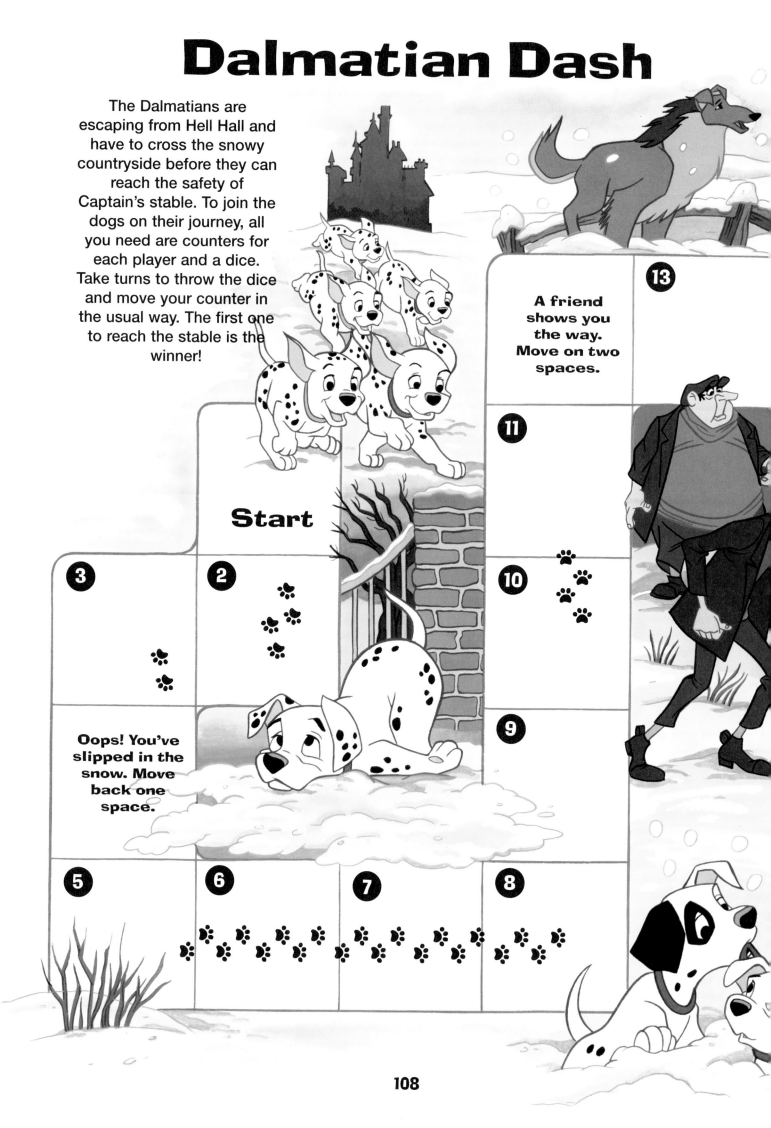

Dalmatian Dash

The Dalmatians are escaping from Hell Hall and have to cross the snowy countryside before they can reach the safety of Captain's stable. To join the dogs on their journey, all you need are counters for each player and a dice. Take turns to throw the dice and move your counter in the usual way. The first one to reach the stable is the winner!

Start

13

A friend shows you the way. Move on two spaces.

11

10

3

2

9

Oops! You've slipped in the snow. Move back one space.

5

6

7

8

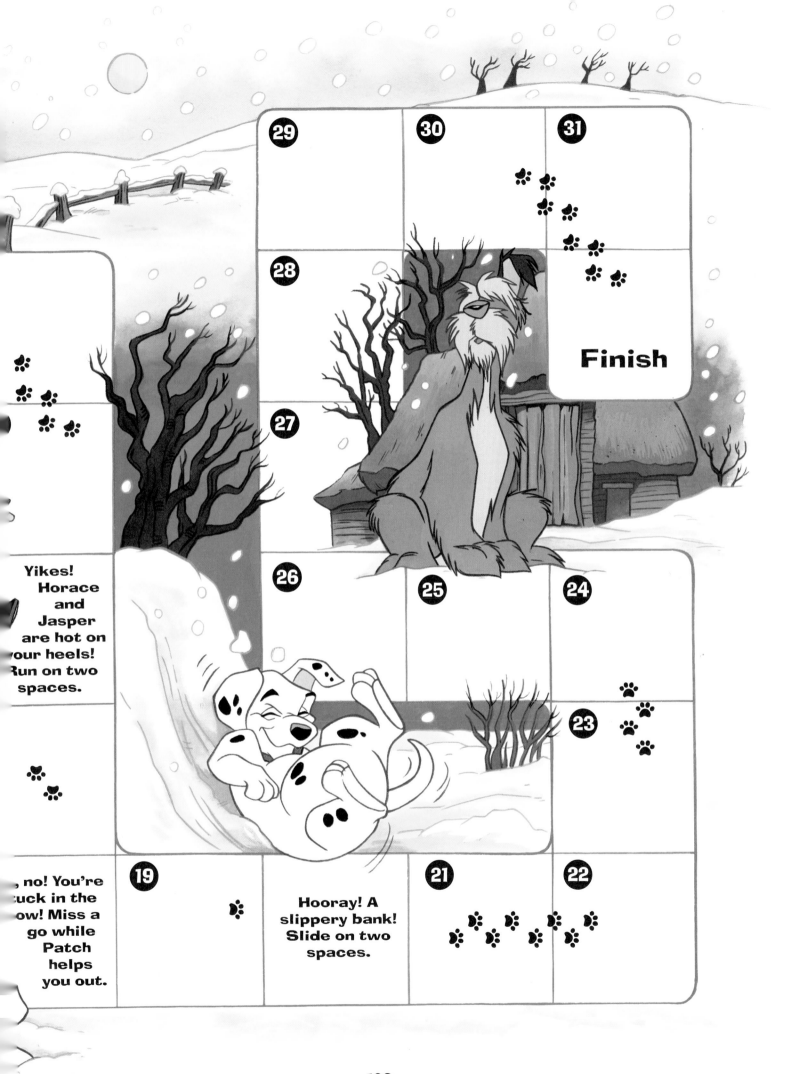

29

30

31

28

27

Finish

Yikes!
Horace
and
Jasper
are hot on
our heels!
Run on two
spaces.

26

25

24

23

no! You're
uck in the
ow! Miss a
go while
Patch
helps
you out.

19

Hooray! A
slippery bank!
Slide on two
spaces.

21

22